Bold Bad Ben the Beastly Bandit

"I am Bold Bad Beastly Ben,
I beat the women and eat the men
I steal your sheets, your shoes, your hair,
And hide them in my mountain lair."

When the townsfolk hear that dreadful song, they lock their doors and huddle in their beds. No one dares even look out of the window to see what he is like until one boy peeps through a keyhole. "He's as tall as a house and has nails down to the ground and the meanest face you ever saw."

The townsfolk were even more scared and Bold Bad Ben got worse and worse. No one knows what to do to stop the monster until the old toymaker takes matters into his own hands.

An amusing moral tale told in comic form with wonderfully funny pictures by Cathy Wilcox.

Other books by Ann Jungman

Ann Jungman and
Cathy Wilcox

Bold Bad

The Beastly Bandit

BARN OWL BOOKS

First published in Australia 1989 by Collins Publishers
55 Clarence Street, Sydney NSW 2000
This edition first published 2003 by Barn Owl Books
157 Fortis Green Road, London N10 3LX
Barn Owl Books are distributed by Frances Lincoln
4 Torriano Mews, Torriano Avenue, London NW5 2RZ

ISBN 1 903015 18 9
A CIP catalogue record for this book
is available from the British Library

Designed and typeset by Douglas Martin, Oadby
Printed in China for Imago

There was once a thriving, peaceful town beside a crystal-clear blue lake in a beautiful lush green valley. It was surrounded by a range of rugged high mountains.

5

The people of the town went about their business cheerfully and all was well.

No-one ever bothered to lock their doors, because they all trusted each other . . .

One day, however, all that changed.
  Bold Bad Ben strode into the
valley and chose a cave high in the
mountains for his beastly bandit
hideout.

From that day life in the town was
different.
   Every night the townspeople would
nervously lock their doors and fasten
their windows.

As the church clock struck twelve,
a terrible noise would be heard as
Bold Bad Ben rode into town singing:

I AM BOLD BAD BEN.
I BEAT THE WOMEN AND EAT THE MEN.
FEE-FI-FO-FUM,
YOU'D BETTER WATCH OUT FOR HERE I COME.
I'LL STEAL YOUR SHEETS, YOUR SHOES, YOUR HAIR,
AND HIDE THEM IN MY MOUNTAIN LAIR!
CLANG!

Bold Bad Ben's evil song terrified
the townspeople.

They hid their heads under the sheets, put their fingers in their ears and prayed that Bold Bad Ben would steal from someone else and go away quickly.

13

Every morning, when the people
woke up, something was missing.

One day it was a cuckoo clock,

another day it was someone's Sunday
roast, or a chicken or a pig.

There was nothing Bold Bad Ben
would not steal – an old kettle,

a broken chair,

a dead plant . . .

Anything that he could lay his evil,
greedy hands on would disappear.

But that was not the worst of it.
Bold Bad Ben was mean and just
loved doing nasty things.

He kicked holes in people's boats.

He threw mud all over a line of
freshly washed sheets.

He cut the ropes that held up the church bells.

Everyone was scared silly with the noise the bells made as they crashed to the ground.

CLANG
CRASH

He smashed the children's toys and threw their bikes into the deepest part of the lake.

19

The townspeople were in despair.

They never knew what would happen next, and all the joy was going out of their lives.

No-one had ever actually seen Bold Bad Ben, for he only prowled around at night.

When the people heard his evil, beastly song they hid shivering inside their locked houses and did not dare to peek out.

Just once, a little boy looked through a keyhole.

He caught a glimpse of a huge hairy monster coming out of the mist. The boy fled, shaking with fear, back to the safety of his bed.

Next day, he reported that Bold Bad
Ben was as tall as two men and as big
as a gorilla, that he had a long black
beard and hairy hands and long nails
that reached down to the ground.

This can't go on!
He's making the cow's milk go sour
He's trampled all the flowers in the park
He stole my false teeth!
As big as a gorilla?!
Like King Kong?!
That monster is ruining our lives!
We must go and see the mayor.

This news made the people even more worried and unhappy. They decided to hold a meeting.

Everyone talked a lot at the
meeting, but no-one had any
ideas about what to do.

They were so busy arguing
that no-one noticed when the
old toymaker left.

Crunch
Crunch

He set off with his horse and cart,
travelling towards the mountains
to look for Bold Bad Ben's hideout.

As the old toymaker and his horse
climbed higher into the bleak
mountains, storm clouds gathered
overhead. Then lightning flashed
through the sky and thunder
rumbled loudly.

BOOMM

CCRRAC

'Well, my, my,' said the old man to his horse. 'I think we'll have to shelter for a while. Ah, I see a cave. How fortunate. Let's go in there.'

Now, just by chance, the cave that the old man had chosen for shelter was the very same one used by Big Bad Ben as his beastly bandit's lair.

31

The old toymaker got down from the
cart and slipped off the horse's harness.
Then he led the horse into the cave.

The cave was dark and smelled musty.

The old man patted his horse on the
nose and looked for somewhere to
sit down.

'It looks as though we're going to
be here for some time,' he explained.
'So we might as well get comfortable.'

At that moment Bold Bad Ben the beastly bandit emerged . . .

. . . from the murky depths of his cave.

The old toymaker did not recognise
him at first, since the bandit was even
shorter than the old man himself.

   Not only that, but Bold Bad Ben was
as thin as a reed, with wispy hair,
frightened eyes and a bad cold.
He didn't look at all frightening.

Bold Bad Ben tried to sound fierce
and wicked as he shouted at the old
man.

'Get out of here before I count to
three or I'll shoot you and that
horrible horse.'

But the old man seemed to be
a bit deaf.

'How kind of you. Did you hear that?'
he asked his horse. 'The dear boy has
offered me a cup of tea.'

Bold Bad Ben didn't know what to do.
He lowered his gun.

He did not really want to shoot the
old man (anyway, his gun was not
loaded). Actually, he was glad to
have company, since he was terrified
by the thunder.

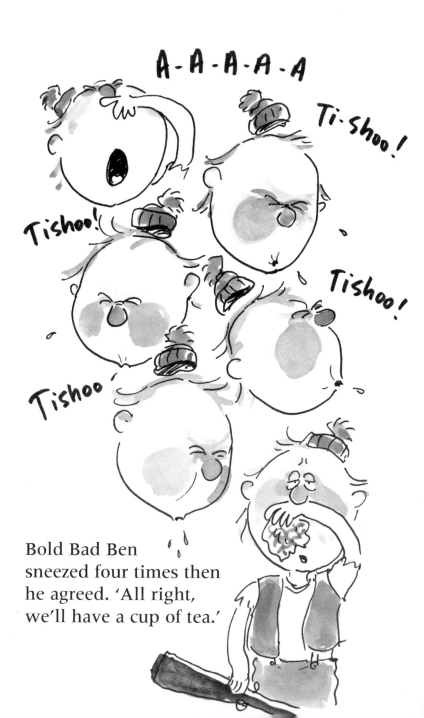

Bold Bad Ben
sneezed four times then
he agreed. 'All right,
we'll have a cup of tea.'

'Bless you, my boy,' said the old man.
'Dearie me, you have a bad cold.
You should be in bed.'

'I know,' sniffed Bold Bad Ben,
feeling very sorry for himself.

'You just show me where things are
  kept in this cave and I'll have a cup of
  tea ready in half a minute,' said the
  old man.
    Walking further into the cave, the
old toymaker looked around.

The cave was piled high with all the things the bandit had stolen.

'My goodness, what a lot of rubbish you have here. Whatever do you do with all these things?' asked the old man.

'Nothing,' muttered the bandit. 'And
you put that down!'

'Town? Yes, of course, dear boy,' he said.

'All these things come from the town. I recognise them all. I wonder how they got here?'

'You sound all stuffed up,' said the old man. 'You really should go and lie down while I make the tea.'

Bold Bad Ben had another sneezing fit and decided to do as the old man said.

He got into his dirty, crumpled bed and pulled the grey, grimy sheet up to his nose.

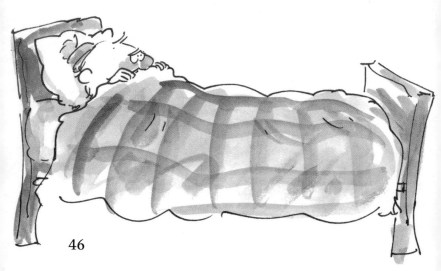

A few minutes later, the old man
came back with two steaming cups
of tea.

'You know, said the old man, 'we must have stumbled into Bold Bad Ben's cave. Do you think that beastly bandit's still there?'

Ben pulled the sheet up so that only the top of his head showed. He shook his head.

'What's that? You drove him off, did you say? You must be very brave for such a little fellow. Most people wouldn't like to tackle Bold Bad Ben alone.'

'Oh dear, what a cold you've got! said the old man. 'Here, drink up!'

A -A- A -A - tishoo
A - tishoo
A - tishoo
A - tishoo

Ben sneezed another four times.

GLUG
GLUG -
SLURP
GLUG

Ben drank the tea gratefully.

How about a bucket of water for me ?!

'What's your name?' asked the old toymaker.

Ben looked up nervously and muttered, 'I'm afraid that . . .'

'Fred?' interrupted the old man. 'Yes, it suits you. Fearless Fred. Wait till the town hears about your heroic deed!'

'Tell me, Fred, you've seen this beastly bandit Bold Bad Ben. Why do you think he stole all these useless things from the town?'

'I don't think he knew why,' said
Ben,'Perhaps he felt left out. Maybe
nobody liked him or took any notice
of him. He might have felt that if he
couldn't be part of everything he
would destroy it.'

  'Yes,' said the old man. 'I suppose
that was it. Poor old Ben. Still, I'm
glad he's gone.'

'You know,' said the old toymaker as Ben got out of bed, 'you remind me of my son. Since he moved away I have no-one to help me in my toymaking business. Would you be interested in a job helping me to make toys?'

Ben thought for a moment, then nodded his head.

'Excellent, excellent. Well, my boy, we'll load up my cart with all Bold Bad Ben's loot and then we can go back to town together. My goodness, won't everyone be happy when they hear that you've driven away that beastly bandit. You'll be a hero.'

Ben thought about it and decided he liked the idea.

So he helped the old man to load up
the cart.

As soon as the storm was over, they set
off for town.

It all happened just as the old man
had said.

The townspeople were overjoyed to hear that the bandit had gone.

They rang the
church bells (which
had sturdy new
ropes) and held a
feast to celebrate.

Before long, Bold Bad Ben the beastly bandit had become a very happy Fred the toymaker.

But for ever after, if anyone
mentioned the terrible times
when Bold Bad Ben the beastly
bandit had terrified the town
(as they often did),

CREEP
CREEP

Fred would walk
away, blushing.

Just one thing worried Fred.

   'Why is it,' he asked the old toymaker, 'that you seem to hear perfectly well now, when you were quite deaf that day in the cave?'

'It must have been the thunder,'
said the old man, and he smiled as
he fixed the sails on the toy boat
he was making.